Little Science Stars

The Weather

The Best Start in Science

By Helen Orme

North American copyright © *ticktock* Entertainment Ltd 2009

First published in North America in 2009 by *ticktock* Media Ltd,
The Old Sawmill, 103 Goods Station Road, Tunbridge Wells, Kent, TN1 2DP, UK

ticktock project editor: Rob Cave
ticktock project designer: Trudi Webb

ISBN-13: 978 1 84696 195 3 pbk

Printed in China
9 8 7 6 5 4 3 2 1

Picture credits (t=top, b=bottom, c=center, l=left, r=right,
OFC=outside front cover, OBC=outside back cover):

iStock: 12b, 20b. NASA: 23t. Shutterstock: OFCt all, 1 all, 2, 3 all,
4-5 all, 6 all, 7 all, 8 all, 9 all, 10 all, 11 all, 12t, 13 all, 14 all, 15 all, 16 all, 17 all,
18 all, 19 all, 20t, 20c, 21 all, 22-23 main, 22 all, 23c, 23b, 24 all, OBC both.

Every effort has been made to trace the copyright holders and we apologize in
advance for any unintentional omissions. We would be pleased to insert the
appropriate acknowledgements in any subsequent edition of this publication.

Contents

Any words appearing in the text in bold, **like this**,
are explained in the Glossary.

Take a look out of your window. Weather is all around us. What is the weather like today?

A cloudy day   A sunny day   A windy day

Sometimes the weather makes you feel hot and
sometimes it makes you feel very cold.

But do you know what
makes it **thunder**?

Or what rainbows are made of?

What makes our weather?

5

How does the Sun make weather?

Lots of things make our weather the way it is, but the Sun is the most important.

The Sun makes heat and light. It warms up the **Earth** where we live.

Without the Sun we would not have sunshine!

North Pole, a cold place

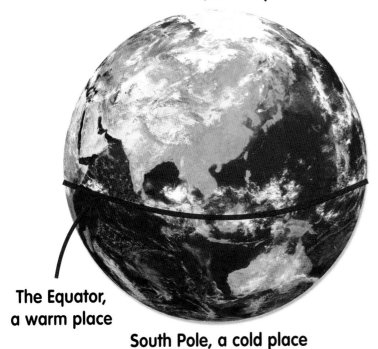

The Equator,
a warm place

South Pole, a cold place

The land and sea around the middle of the Earth at the **Equator** get hotter than the land and sea at the **Poles**.

The warm air and sea at the Equator moves from the hottest places towards the colder ones.

When this happens different types of weather are made.

Antarctica (the South Pole) is one of the coldest places on Earth.

What are clouds made of?

Clouds look **solid**, but they are made up of millions of tiny drops of water and **ice crystals**.

These water drops and ice crystals are so small that they float and move in the air.

Clouds with sharp edges are made of water droplets, while those with fuzzy edges are made of ice crystals.

Clouds close
to the ground
are called **fog**.

Clouds sometimes
cover the Sun,
stopping the
sunshine.

It might even rain!

Why does it rain?

Clouds bring rain. In the clouds tiny drops of water join together.

When the drops get too big they are too heavy to stay in the air.

Then **raindrops** fall out of the clouds!

People wear special clothes when it rains so they don't get wet.

In some countries rain comes at special times of the year, called monsoon.

Monsoon rain is very heavy and lasts for days.

Floods caused by monsoon rain

How often does it rain where you live?

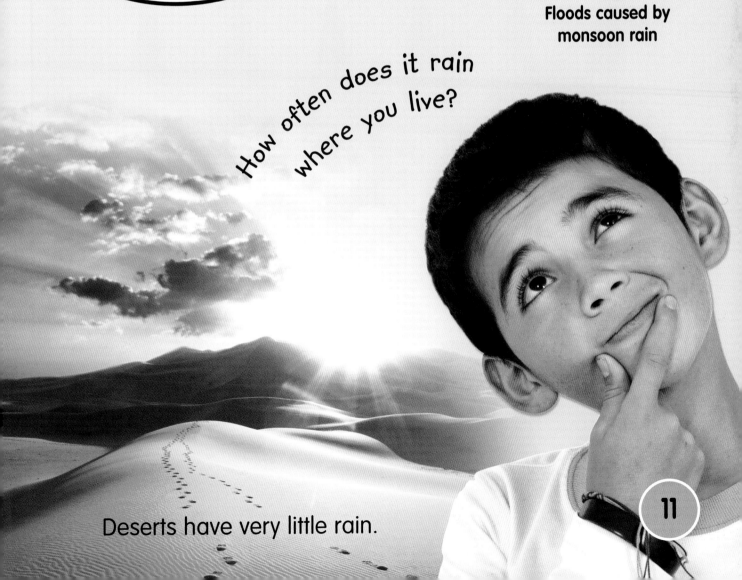

Deserts have very little rain.

11

What are rainbows made of?

Rainbows are made of colored light.

If there are still water drops in the air after rain and the Sun comes out, a rainbow will appear.

The colors of a rainbow always appear in the same order – red, orange, yellow, green, blue, indigo and violet.

Sunlight shines through the raindrops and comes out as bands of colored light. When this happens we see a rainbow.

It is impossible to reach the end of a rainbow.

Make your own rainbows by holding a **CD** out in sunlight. The shiny CD splits **rays of light** in the same way a drop of water does.

What are hail and snow made of?

Ice crystals

Some rain starts as ice crystals. In warm air most of these **frozen** drops **melt** into rain.

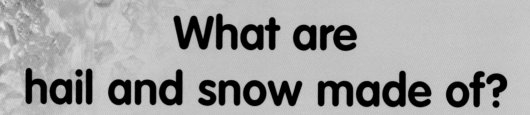

But if the ice crystals are very big, they don't melt and we get **hail**.

In winter the air is often so cold that even small ice crystals won't melt.

These small crystals stick together to make **snow**.

No two **snowflakes** are alike.

If the ground is cold the snow will **settle**.

Time for some fun, but wrap up warm!

Hat

What makes the wind blow?

You can't see **wind**, but you can see what it does.

It blows the leaves off trees and makes their branches move around.

Wind happens when air moves.

The wind even moves clouds in the sky.

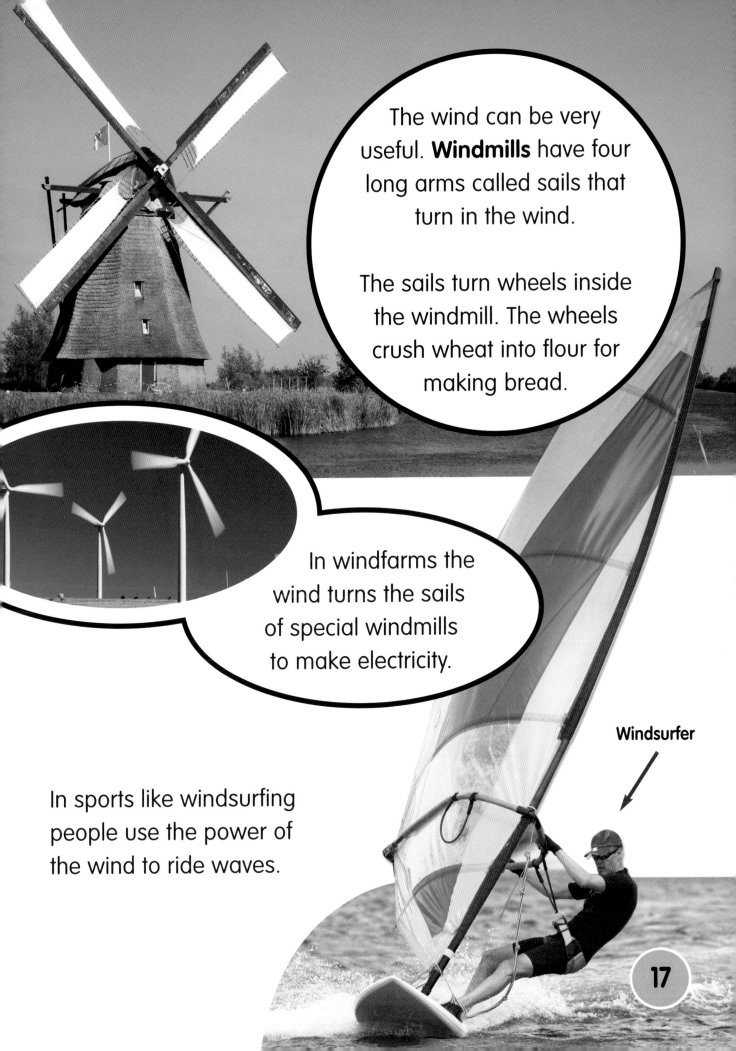

The wind can be very useful. **Windmills** have four long arms called sails that turn in the wind.

The sails turn wheels inside the windmill. The wheels crush wheat into flour for making bread.

In windfarms the wind turns the sails of special windmills to make electricity.

In sports like windsurfing people use the power of the wind to ride waves.

Windsurfer

17

How strong can the wind blow?

Wind can be useful, but sometimes it is so strong it becomes frightening.

Trees sometimes lose their branches in fall **gales**.

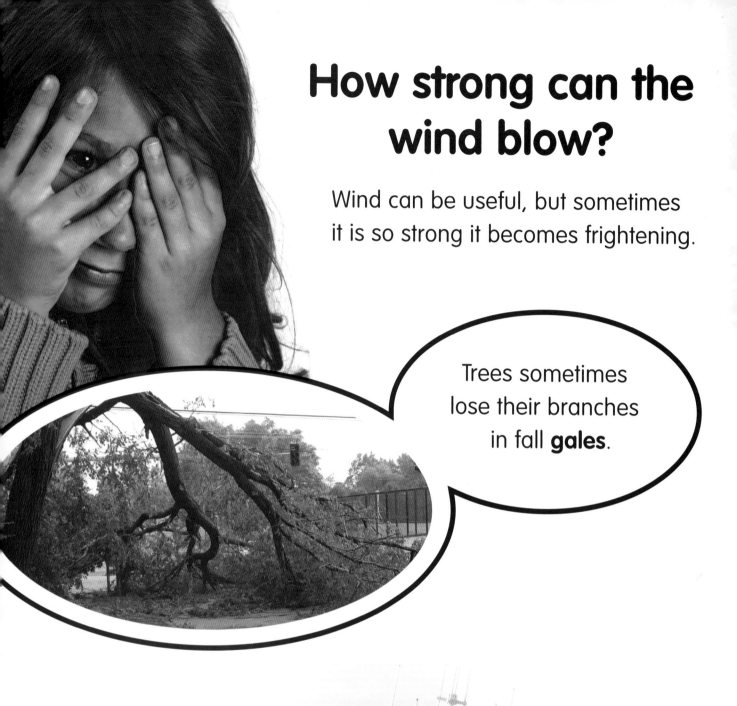

Hurricanes are strong wind storms. They start out at sea, and they can travel great distances.

They do a lot of damage on land.

Hurricanes can blow cars into the air and rip the roofs off houses.

Tornadoes are made of spinning wind. They look like funnels of dark clouds in the sky.

Tornadoes move very quickly. Like hurricanes, they wreck buildings.

What causes thunder and lightning?

Thunderstorms often happen when the air gets very hot.

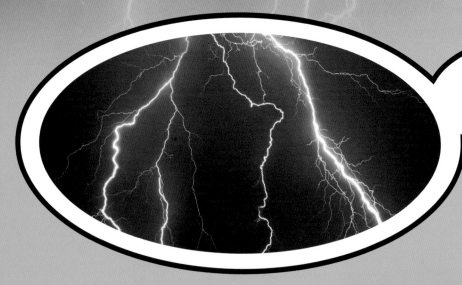

Electricity is produced in thunderclouds.

A tree struck by lightning

We see this electricity as flashes of lightning.

If a **lightning bolt** hits something, it can cause a lot of damage. It strikes the highest object it finds. That can be a tree, a building or a person. Beware!

Lightning moves very quickly, heating up the air on the way. This causes thunder.

Thunder is the loud noise that air makes when it becomes very hot, very quickly.

Sometimes you get heavy rainfall with a thunderstorm.

Questions and answers

Q What are rainbows made of?

A Rainbows are made of colored light.

Q Why does lightning come before thunder?

A Because light travels faster than sound.

Q What causes thunder and lightning?

A Electricity causes thunder and lightning.

Q What makes the wind blow?

A Moving air makes the wind blow.

Q Is the Sun bigger than the Earth?

A Yes, the Sun is much bigger than the Earth.

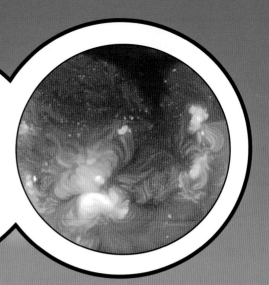

Q How can snow cause sunburn?

A Sunlight can burn your skin. Snow reflects sunlight very well.

Q What are hail and snow made of?

A Hail and snow are made of ice crystals.

Q What are clouds made of?

A Clouds are made of tiny drops of water and ice crystals.

Glossary

CD A compact disc.

Clouds Masses of water drops floating in the sky.

Earth The planet we live on.

Equator An imaginary line round the middle of the Earth. It cuts the Earth into north and south. It is very hot at the Equator.

Fog Clouds on the ground that make it difficult to see.

Frozen A liquid (like water) that has got so cold it has become solid and turned to ice.

Gales Strong winds.

Hail Small pieces of ice that fall to the ground.

Hurricanes Very strong winds.

Ice crystals Frozen raindrops.

Lightning bolt A single flash of electricity produced inside clouds. You see lightning bolts in the sky.

Melt When a solid turns into a liquid—usually because it has been heated. When ice is heated it melts and turns to water.

Poles The North and South Poles are the places that are furthest away from the equator. It is very cold at the poles.

Rays of light Light that is moving in a straight line.

Raindrops Water from the clouds which falls as rain.

Settle Collect on the ground.

Snow Lots of tiny falling ice crystals.

Snowflake A single flake of snow.

Solid Something that can be touched or held.

Thunder The sound made by lightning flashes.

Thunderstorms A storm where there is thunder and lightning.

Tornadoes Columns of spinning wind.

Wind Moving air.

Windmills Buildings with big sails that turn in the wind. The sails turn wheels that can be used to crush grain, or make electricity.

Index

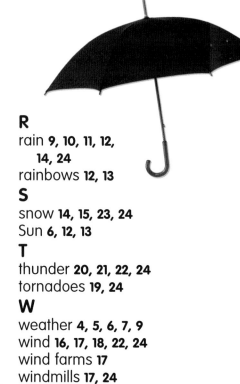